CW00840170

Piper and Pooka

Other Orchard Storybooks

for John —
all good wishes

Kevin Crossley-Holland

BOGGARTS AND BOGLES

Piper and Pooka

Kevin
Crossley-Holland

Illustrated by
Peter Melnyczuk

ORCHARD BOOKS
London

Text copyright © Kevin Crossley-Holland 1988
Illustrations copyright © Peter Melnyczuk 1988
First published in Great Britain in 1988 by
ORCHARD BOOKS
10 Golden Square, London W1R 3AF
Orchard Books Australia
14 Mars Road, Lane Cove NSW 2066
Orchard Books Canada
20 Torbay Road, Markham, Ontario 23P 1G6
1 85213 093 8
Typeset in Great Britain by
Tradespools Limited, Frome, Somerset
Printed in Great Britain by
A. Wheaton, Exeter
Adapted from *British Folk Tales*
by Kevin Crossley-Holland,
published by Orchard Books

Contents

The Piper
and The Pooka

The only tune that Patsy could play was "Black Rogue". He put a pillow of wind in his bagpipe and he played it loud and played it soft; he played it for all he was worth and on every occasion.

The trouble was that Patsy was as dim as a donkey. Much as he loved music and dancing, he was unable to learn more than one tune. When at a dance someone called on him to play another tune, he'd smile and strike it up only to frown and break off after a few snatches, shaking his head and muttering to himself, "It's gone. Where's it gone?"

Late one night, Patsy was walking home after playing at a dance in a neighbouring village. It wasn't too friendly a way, what with hanging rocks on either side of the road, and it wasn't too friendly a night — dungeon-dark and the November wind whistling sharp and out of tune.

Weaving down the tiddly road, Patsy felt a little lonely; and when he reached the hump-backed bridge, he was still two miles out from the village of Dunmore and the warmth of his mother's cottage. So he unstrung his pipes and put wind in the bag and began to play.

Up behind the piper crept a

shape. The shape had horns. First it was two-legged, now it was four-legged. It grinned and it lowered its head.

"Wowk!" shouted Patsy, as first

he felt the horns jammed against his buttocks and then he lost his footing and was tossed into the air.

Patsy did a backwards somersault and landed on the creature's back. He got a good grip on its horns and yelled, "The devil take you, you nasty beast! Let me go home!"

"Never mind home," said the creature.

"I've been playing all night," shouted Patsy. "I've got a sixpenny piece for my pains, and it's for my mother."

"Never mind your mother!" said the creature.

"She needs it to buy snuff," cried Patsy.

"Stuff!" replied the creature. "You just keep a hold on my horns. If you fall off, you'll break your pipes — and you'll break your neck too."

So Patsy gripped the creature's shaggy back with his knees and before long, as they trotted along, it said, "Play up, Patsy! Play 'Poor Old Woman' for me."

"How can I do that?" said Patsy. "I've never heard of it."

"Never mind whether you have or you haven't," said the creature. "You play up and I'll see you know it."

So the piper put wind in his bag and he began to play. Oh! The darkness lightened and clouds danced in front of the moon; the sharp-tongued wind stood back. Patsy played high and low, simple and difficult. All the listening cows and rabbits and sheep pawed at the ground and stamped, all of them longing to be part of the dance.

At last Patsy came to the end of the tune. The pipes wheezed and fell silent and Patsy took a deep breath. "My!" he said. "You're a fine music master."

The creature said nothing. It kept trotting forward at a steady pace, untroubled by the dark or the piper on its back.

"Where are we going?" asked Patsy. "Will you tell me that?"

"There's a great feast tonight," said the creature, "in the house of the weeping women."

"Where's that, then?" asked Patsy.

"Up on top of the holy mountain," said the creature. "Croagh Patrick."

"Is that right?" said Patsy. "You're saving me a journey, then. Last week I stole Father William's white gander. And when he found out, he told me my punishment was to climb Croagh Patrick."

Now the creature increased the length of his step, and broke into a kind of canter. Round rugged out-crops and over squelching peat bogs, into tapering valleys and up steep slopes — on they went until at last they came to the top of Croagh Patrick.

The creature stopped. He struck the ground three times with one hoof. Then in the half-light Patsy saw a great rock door slowly open, and at once the creature passed through it with the piper still on his back. They entered a great shining hall.

Patsy let go of the creature's horns and slipped off its back and looked about him. In the middle of the room stood a huge table, much the largest Patsy had ever seen in his

life, and it looked as if it were made from gold.

Round the table sat a crowd of old women, there must have been hundreds of them — and all of them had long hair, and eyes red as firecoals from wailing and weeping. They wore green dresses and grey cloaks.

Now there was a great scraping and rustling. The women stood up and called out, "A thousand thousand welcomes to you, Pooka of November! Who is this you've brought with you?"

"The best piper in Ireland," said the Pooka.

One of the old women stepped

towards Patsy, and struck the ground with her stick. At once a little door in the rock wall opened, and out stepped a white gander, the same that Patsy had stolen from Father William.

"My!" said Patsy. "By my conscience, I ate this gander!" The piper eyed the bird and the bird eyed Patsy. "My mother and I, we ate every piece of him—all except one wing, and I gave that to Red Mary. The devil take her, it's she told Father William . . ."

But now the gander seemed to have lost interest in Patsy. It paddled away and started to clear the plates and goblets from the table.

"Now, Patsy," said the Pooka, "you must play up! Play a tune for these ladies."

So Patsy played "Black Rogue",

the only tune he knew, and the old
women began to dance — backward
and forward and round and round,
their grey hair and white hair
streaming out behind them. But
then Patsy struck up a second tune
and a third, a whole succession of
tunes which, like "Poor Old
Woman", he'd never even heard of
before. The old women danced
until they were too tired to dance
any longer.

"Pay the piper, ladies!" shouted
the Pooka, grinning from ear to ear.
"Pay the piper!" The old women
stumbled and fumbled as each and
every one of them found a gold coin
in a purse, or hidden pocket, and
gave it to Patsy.

"Bags of it!" brayed Patsy. "By the tooth of St. Patrick, I'm as rich as the son of a lord."

"Come with me," said the Pooka. "I'll take you home."

Patsy and the Pooka turned towards the door and, just as the piper was about to mount once more on the creature's back, the white gander prinked up to Patsy and presented him with a brand new set of pipes.

"That's very handsome," said Patsy. "Very polite! I wish I hadn't eaten you."

It wasn't long before the Pooka brought Patsy back to the little hump-backed bridge only two miles outside the village of Dunmore.

"Go home, Patsy!" said the creature, and its black eyes gleamed in the light of dawn. "You've got two things now you didn't have before."

"What's that?" asked Patsy.

"Some wits between your two ears," said the Pooka, "and a memory for music."

So Patsy strode home to his mother's cottage and, in the first pale green light, banged on the door. And when his sleeping mother took more than a moment to rouse herself, Patsy banged again and bawled, "Let me in! Let me in! I'm as rich as a lord and the best piper in Ireland."

"I'll tell you what you are," said Patsy's mother. "You're as drunk as a lord, and a rogue into the bargain."

"Not at all," said Patsy. "I haven't drunk a drop. Not a drop since midnight."

Patsy's mother opened the door and let her son in. Then she crossed the little room and knelt down in front of the dozy fire and cupped her hands and began to blow at the peats.

"Look!" said Patsy, emptying his pockets. "There!" he shouted, as the gold pieces ran all over the floor.

"Patsy!" cried his mother. "Where in heaven's name . . ." The old woman scrambled to left and to right, gathering up all the pieces of gold so that they lay in one shining pool in her lap.

"And these new pipes!" said

Patsy proudly. "Wait now till you hear the music I play."

Patsy buckled on the pipes and filled the bag with wind. But what music! Instead of responding to his quick fingers, the pipes made a hideous cackling, as if all the ganders and geese in Ireland were tucked inside them and cackling together.

"Stop!" shouted Patsy's mother. "Stop!"

Patsy needed no encouragement. He unstrapped the pipes and put them in the corner of the little room. But the terrible racket had already woken up all the neighbours in the surrounding cottages. Tipsy with sleep and tousled, they came stumbling through the door one after another, first indignant, then curious, then mocking.

"I'll put on my old pipes then," said Patsy stubbornly.

"And play 'Black Rogue'!" said several voices, none too kindly. "'Black Rogue', Patsy! Is that what you'll do?"

But Patsy did not play "Black Rogue". He closed his eyes and opened his eyes and his fingers remembered all the dances and every note that he played for the weeping women on the top of Croagh Patrick.

"And then there's this," said Patsy's mother slyly, untying the shawl in which she had secreted all the gold, and laying it out in front of her friends and neighbours.

21

Then Patsy himself sat down in front of the laughing fire and told them everything that had happened since he left the dance the previous night. "All of it," he said, "while you were asleep. All of it between midnight and first light."

After they had eaten later that morning, Patsy's mother had a peep into the shawl for the second time. It was full of crackling leaves, nothing but November leaves, russet and gold and brown.

"Ah! Patsy!" said his mother sadly, and with one clump of a fist she covered her eyes.

Then Patsy went to find Father William and told him everything that had happened the previous night.

Father William shook his head.

He kept shaking his head and he smiled. "Cock and bull!" he said. "Claptrap, Patsy! And you know it."

"It's true," said Patsy, indignantly. "I'll show you. I'll put these pipes on me." He buckled on the new pipes and filled the bag till it was bursting. Once more the pipes made a horrible honking and screeching.

"Get out, you thief!" shouted Father William.

"And now these," said Patsy, as soon as the caterwauling had died away.

"Out!" shouted Father William. "Away with you! And off to Croagh Patrick!"

But Patsy stood his ground and fastened on his old pipes. And then what music he played! First he played well-known tunes, and then the unfamiliar tunes he had played for the weeping women at the top of the mountain — and all with neat fingering and fine phrasing, true to the circle of the dance.

The old priest clicked his fingers and inside his shiny black shoes his toes began to tingle. Little birds looked in at his window.

And from that day until the day he died, Patsy was hailed as prince of pipers in the county of Galway.

The Farmer and The Boggart

Terry was very pleased to be able to buy Far Wallow. True, it wasn't much more than an acre, and the bottom end, down towards the stream, was a bit sticky, but all the same it meant he could provide for his growing family all the year round.

"And there might be something left over at that," he told his wife. "Something to sell."

On the evening the purchase was

completed, Terry lit his pipe and strolled down Far Wallow to the stream. He put one foot on the stump of an old willow tree; he listened to the mouthing of the stream; he rubbed the bridge of his nose, and closed his eyes. He looked just what he was: a man at peace with the world, savouring the particular satisfaction of owning land.

When Terry opened his eyes again, he saw a little man advancing down Far Wallow towards him. And then he saw his visitor was a squat boggart; his whole face was covered in hair and his arms were almost as long as walking-sticks.

"Clear off my land!" said the boggart.

"Your land!" exclaimed Terry. "I've just bought it."

"No," said the boggart. "That's mine."

"It's not," said Terry.

"That is," said the boggart.

"It's not," said Terry.

"That's mine. That's always been mine."

"I've just signed the papers," said Terry.

The boggart scratched his hairy chin, looking as much puzzled as threatening. "I'm sure that's mine," he said.

"I'll take you to court," said Terry.

"Court!" said the boggart, and he spat at Terry's feet. "I'll take half

27

what you grow. That's what."

Terry didn't like the boggart's
suggestion at all, but he didn't want
to upset him. One clout from his
hairy right arm and he would be
down in the stream.

"Well?" said the boggart.

"All right," said Terry slowly.
"Right. What do you want, tops or
bottoms?"

The boggart scratched the back
of his head. "Tops or bottoms?" he
repeated.

"Above ground or beneath
ground?"

"Tops," said the boggart.

"Right," said Terry again. "No back-reckonings, mind!"

"Tops," said the boggart and he stumped away.

The year became glum. The silver leaves from the willow trees danced and spun; winter opened her white fan.

In the spring, Terry planted the whole of Far Wallow with potatoes. And when it was late July and time to lift them, the boggart came stumping back to the field to claim his share.

"Right!" said Terry. "No back-reckonings, mind!"

So of course Terry got the whole potato crop and the boggart was left with nothing but leaves and stalks.

"Blast!" shouted the boggart in frustration, as Terry loaded his crop on to a cart. "Blast! Next year..."

"Yes?" said Terry.

"What was it?"

"Tops?" said Terry.

"No!" said the boggart, looking worried.

"Bottoms," said Terry.

"That's it! Bottoms!"

"Right," said Terry. "No back-reckonings, mind!"

First Terry ploughed and har-

rowed Far Wallow; then he sowed it with wheat. So when the boggart came the following August to claim his share, he was left with nothing but stubble and Terry got all the corn and straw.

"Blast!" shouted the boggart.

"Blast!" Then he turned on Terry. "Next year," he said, "you sow wheat and we'll mow side by side. Each to take what he mows."

"Ah!" said Terry.

"I'll start down here and you start up there," said the boggart. "That's what!" he bellowed in Terry's right ear. And then he stumped away, muttering to himself.

Before long, Terry went to see

the wise man. "I've outwitted him twice," said Terry. "But what am I to do this third time?"

"Sow the field with wheat," said the wise man, "and during the winter, have the blacksmith make you a hundred thin iron rods. Then, in the spring, when the wheat rises, plant the rods in Far Wallow. Plant them all over the part where the boggart wants to mow. That'll soon wear down his strength and take the edge off his scythe."

Terry did as the wise man advised him. The days lengthened, the wheat strengthened and turned pale yellow, pale rose, tawny.

The boggart came back in the middle of August to claim his share.

"I'll start down here and you start up there," said the boggart.

"I remember," said Terry.

So the boggart swung his scythe, and before long he hit one of the iron rods.

"Rum old stalks," grumbled the boggart. "Rum old stalks, aren't they?"

But Terry kept scything and pre-

tending not to hear. So the boggart
had to stop and whet his scythe.
And no sooner had he put a new

edge on it, than he struck another
iron rod.

"Blast!" shouted the boggart.
"Far Wallow never was up to
much."

Terry leant on his scythe and
listened.

"You can take the mucky old
land and the crops on it," shouted
the boggart. "I won't have no more
to do with it." And with that the
hairy creature plodded away, over
the stile and out of sight, without so

much as a backward look.

For months after that, the bog-gart hung around the dykes and drains that ran between the fields in the fen; sometimes he scared people walking home alone late at night; and if a farmer left his dinner or his tools in the corner of some far field, he sometimes sneaked up and made off with them. But the years passed and the boggart never came near Far Wallow again.

Hughbo

The only house on the little island was low-slung and whitewashed. In stormy weather it was swept by saltspray, and in every season scolded by wind; and that was where Peter lived on his own.

For as long as it was light, he worked the land. He ploughed and sowed and reaped as his father and mother had done before their drowning; he made hay, he milked his cows and cut the peats. And

35

each Sunday morning, he rowed over to the mainland to visit his sweetheart.

In the evenings, Peter lit candles in his kitchen and sat yawning beside the fire. Through the door, in the stable, he could hear the lowing of his cows and the snuffling of his pigs as they settled down for the night.

One night, when the wind was going wild outside, the young farmer climbed into his box-bed and was just about to blow out the candle when he saw the dark corner beside the stable door was gleaming. Peter looked more carefully, and made out the figure of a little crouching man. He was naked from head to toe, and his leathery brown skin shone in the dark.

"Lord!" said the farmer, and he

gripped the sides of his bed, not for one moment taking his eyes off the ugly creature—his squashed nose and puffy lips and large ears, the flat bald crown of his head, his stringy seaweed hair and beard.

Then Peter jumped out of bed. With one hand he grabbed his prayerbook, and with the other he picked up his cut-throat razor.

"Hughbo! I'm Hughbo! Hughbo!" said the creature.

The farmer crossed himself with the prayerbook, and made a circle in the air with his razor.

The ugly creature didn't move. He didn't step forward into the kitchen or back through the door into the stable. He just watched the young man and repeated, "I'm Hughbo!"

Then Peter picked up the iron poker and tongs and threw them at the creature. But the little man ducked the first and side-stepped the second.

Peter was afraid and angry. He unhooked the metal pot hanging from its chain above the fire and with both hands started to swing it . . .

At this the little man darted forward. He grabbed the rim of the pot.

"Get out!" shouted Peter, swinging both fists and catching the crea-

ture one blow on his ribs and another on the back of his head.

But the little man was as light on his feet as a cat. He leaped across the kitchen and, with a yell, disappeared through the stable door.

Peter rubbed his eyes, and wondered what to do. And within a minute, the ugly creature crept back into the corner of the kitchen and started grinning at him.

"I'm Hughbo!" said the creature, and he pointed to himself.

"What do you want?" said Peter.

"I live in the ocean."

"What do you want here?"

"Sick and tired of chewing dead men's bones," said the creature.

"Do you want bread?" asked Peter.

The creature grinned. "I'll work for my lodging."

"I said nothing about lodging," Peter replied, looking at the creature's leathery skin and seaweed hair.

But the ugly little man went on grinning. "Hughbo work well! Every night I'll grind the corn."

Peter narrowed his eyes. Busy that he was, he wasn't sorry at the offer of help. *I'll judge him by his work*, he thought, *not by his looks!*

And so the young farmer agreed that Hughbo would grind the corn each night and make enough meal for the farmer's morning plate of porridge. In return, Peter allowed Hughbo to sleep on the threshold between the kitchen and the stable, and to take one saucer of milk each morning to add to his own supply of parched barley.

That same night, Peter lay in bed

and watched the gleaming creature in the corner of the kitchen; he closed his eyes and fell asleep to the skirl of the wind.

In the morning, the farmer was well pleased with his clean, sharply ground corn. And after only a few days, he began to feel quite at home with his strange sea-visitor, and to welcome his company.

Each Sunday, when he rowed over to the mainland to see her, Peter told Janey more about Hugh-bo — his friendliness and readiness to work and dependability.

"I don't know how I'd manage without him," said the young man. And twice he rowed Janey out to

the island so that she could see Hughbo for herself.

"All leather and kelp and not a stitch of clothing," Janey exclaimed. "And that gleam! I'll never get used to him."

"I have," said Peter.

One summer day the young farmer married Janey and brought her back to his little wind-loud island. How happy they were! At first light they rose and, after cooking the corn Hughbo had ground for them, they worked in the fields together; in the afternoon, Janey stayed in the farm, and cleaned and sewed and cooked; and when Peter came in at dusk, they ate supper and talked and laughed; they sat close to each other in front of the fire; they went to bed early.

Hughbo always took care not to

disturb Peter and Janey, and ate his food in the stable, and when Janey saw him standing alone and naked, she began to feel sorry for him.

"The nights are getting chill,"

she said to herself. "If my man cares for Hughbo, I must care for him too."

On her next visit to the mainland, Janey bought some cloth. During the next week she cut out and sewed a fine cloak for Hughbo with a hood to cover his bald head. "That should please him," she said to herself, "and please my man too."

When it was finished, Janey spread the cloak on the floor, just before getting into bed.

"What are you doing?" asked the young man.

"Coming to bed!" said Janey.

As usual, Hughbo entered the kitchen quietly so as not to disturb the young man and his wife. But as soon as he saw the new cloak, Hughbo began to moan and to sob.

Peter and Janey sat up in the dark.

"Hughbo!" said Peter. "Hughbo! What's wrong?"

Round and round the little man stumped, sobbing and saying again and again:

"Hughbo's got a cloak and hood,
   So Hughbo can do no more good.
   Hughbo's got a cloak and hood,
   So Hughbo can do no more good."

Then, without even looking in the direction of the young man and his wife, Hughbo threw open the farm-house door and plunged out into the wind and the darkness. And search for him as they did, Peter and Janey, they never saw Hughbo again.

Tom Tit Tot

There was once a little old village where a woman lived with her dizzy daughter. The daughter was just sixteen, and sweet as honeysuckle.

One fine morning, the woman made five meat pies and put them in the oven. But then a neighbour called round and they were soon so busy with snippets of gossip that the woman completely forgot about the pies. By the time she took them out of the oven, their crusts were almost as hard as the bark of her old oak tree.

"Daughter," she said, "you put them there pies in the larder."

"My! I'm that hungry," said the girl.

"Leave them there and they'll come again."

"Come again?"

"You know," said the woman. And she hurried out into the warm wind and her waiting neighbour.

"Well!" said the girl. "If they'll come again, I'll eat these now." And so she went back to the larder and picked up the pies and ate them all, first and last.

When it was supper time, the woman felt very hungry. "I could just do with one of them there pies," she said. "Go and get one off the shelf. They'll have come again now."

The girl went and looked in the larder, and there was nothing on the shelf but an empty dish. "No!" she called. "They haven't."

"Not none of them?" said the woman.

"No!" the girl called. "No! Not none."

"Well!" said the woman. "Come again or not, I'll have one for my supper."

"You can't if they haven't come," said the girl, walking out of the larder.

"I can though," said the woman. "Go and get the best one."

48

"Best or worst," said the girl, "I've eaten the lot, so you can't have one till that's come again."

The woman was furious. "Eaten the lot!" she cried. "You dardle-dumdue!"

The woman carried her spinning wheel over to the door and, to calm herself, she began to spin. As she spun she sang:

"My daughter's ate five;
   five pies today.
My daughter's ate five;
   five pies today."

The king came walking down the street and heard the woman. "What were those words, woman?" he asked. "What were you singing?"

The woman felt ashamed of her daughter's greed. "Well!" she said, beginning to spin again:

"My daughter's spun five;
five skeins today.
My daughter's spun five;
five skeins today."

"Stars of mine!" exclaimed the king. "I've never heard of anyone who could do that." The king raised his eyebrows and looked at the girl, so sweet and dizzy and sixteen; he stared at a flowerbed and rubbed his nose.

"Five today," said the woman.

"Look here!" said the king. "I want a wife and I'll marry your daughter. For eleven months of the year," he said, "she can eat as much food as she likes, and buy all the dresses she wants; she can keep whatever company she wishes. But during the last month of the year, she'll have to spin five skeins of wool every day; and if she doesn't, I'll cut off her head."

"All right!" said the woman. "That's all right, isn't it, daughter?"

The woman was delighted at the thought that her daughter was going to marry the king himself.

51

She wasn't worried about the five skeins of wool. "When that comes to it," she told her daughter later, "we'll find a way out of it. More likely, though, he'll have clean forgot about it."

So the king and the girl were married. And for eleven months the girl ate as much food as she liked and bought all the dresses she wanted and kept whatever company she wished.

As the days of the eleventh month passed, the girl began to think about those skeins of wool and wondered whether the king was thinking about them too. But the king said not a word, and the girl was almost sure he had completely forgotten them.

On the very last day of the month, though, the king led her up to a room in the palace she had never set eyes on before. There was

nothing in it but a spinning wheel and a stool.

"Now, my dear," said the king, "you'll be shut in here tomorrow with some food and wool. And if you haven't spun five skeins before dark, your head will be cut off."

Then away went the king to do everything a king has to do.

Well, the girl was that frightened. She had always been such a giddy girl, and she didn't know how to spin. She didn't know what to do next morning, with no one beside her and no one to help her. She sat down on a stool in the palace kitchen and heavens! how she did cry.

All of a sudden, however, she heard a sort of knocking low down on the door. So she stood up and opened the door, and what did she see but a small little black thing with a long tail. It looked up at her, all curious, and it said, "Well! What are you crying for?"

"What's that to you?" sobbed the girl.

"Never you mind," it said. "You tell me what you're crying for."

"That won't do me no good if I do," the girl replied.

"You don't know that," it said, and twirled its tail round.

"Well!" she said. "That won't do me no harm if that don't do me no good." So she told it about the pies and the skeins and everything.

"This is what I'll do," said the little black thing. "I'll come to your window every morning and take the wool; and I'll bring it back all spun before dark."

"What will that cost me?" she asked.

The thing looked out of the corners of its eyes and it said, "Every night I'll give you three guesses at my name. And if you haven't guessed it before the month's up, you shall be mine."

Well, she thought she was bound to guess its name before the month was out. "All right," she said. "I agree to that."

"All right!" it said, and lork! how it twirled its tail.

Well, next morning, the king led the girl up to the room, and the wool and the day's food were all ready for her.

"There's the wool," said her husband, "and if it isn't spun before dark, off goes your head!" Then he went out and locked the door.

The king had scarcely gone out when there was a knocking at the window.

The girl stood up and opened it and, sure enough, there was the

little old thing sitting on the window ledge.

"Where's the wool?" it said.

"Here it is!" she said.

Well, when it was early evening, there was a knocking again at the window. The girl stood up and opened it, and there was the little old thing, with five skeins of wool over his arm.

"Here it is!" it said, and it gave the wool to her. "And now," it said, "what's my name?"

"What, is that Bill?" she said.

"No!" it said, "that ain't." And it twirled its tail.

"Is that Ned?" she said.

"No!" it said, "that ain't." And it twirled its tail.

"Well, is that Mark?" said she.

"No!" it said, "that ain't." And it twirled its tail faster, and away it flew.

Well, when the girl's husband came in, the five skeins were ready for him. "I see I shan't have to kill you tonight, my dear," he said. "You'll have your food and your wool in the morning," he said, and away he went to do everything a king has to do.

Well, the wool and the food were made ready for the girl each day, and each day the little black impet used to come in the morning and return in the early evening. And each day and all day the girl sat thinking of names to try out on the impet when he came back in the evening. But she never hit on the right one! As time went on towards the end of the month, the impet looked wickeder and wickeder, and it twirled its tail faster and faster each time she made a guess.

So they came to the last day of the month but one. The impet returned in the early evening with the five skeins, and it said, "What, hain't you guessed my name yet?"

"Is that Nicodemus?" she said.

"No! 't'ain't," it said.

"Is that Samuel?" she said.

"No! 't'ain't," it said.

"Ah! well. Is that Methusalem?" said she.

"No! 't'ain't that either," it said. And then it looked at the girl with eyes like burning coals.

"Woman," it said, "there's only tomorrow evening, and then you'll be mine!" And away it flew!

Well, the girl felt terrible. Soon, though, she heard the king coming along the passage; and when he had walked into the room and seen the five skeins, he said, "Well, my dear! So far as I can see, you'll have your skeins ready tomorrow evening too. I reckon I won't have to kill you, so I'll have my supper in here tonight." So the king's servants brought up his supper, and another stool for him, and the two of them sat down together.

Well, the king had scarcely eaten

a mouthful before he pushed back his stool, and waved his knife and fork, and began to laugh.

"What is it?" asked the girl.

"I'll tell you," said the king. "I was out hunting today, and I got lost and came to a clearing in the forest I'd never seen before. There was an old chalkpit there. And I heard a kind of sort of humming. So I got off my horse and crept up to the edge of the pit and looked down into it. And do you know what I saw? The funniest little black thing you ever set eyes on! And what did it have but a little spinning wheel! It was spinning and spinning, wonderfully fast, spinning and twirling its tail. And as it spun, it sang,

"Nimmy nimmy not,
My name's Tom Tit Tot."

Well, when the girl heard this, she could have jumped out of her skin for joy; but she didn't say a word.

Next morning, the small little black thing looked wicked as wicked when it came for the wool. And just before it grew dark, she heard it knocking again at the window pane. She opened the window and it came right in on to the sill. It was grinning from ear to ear, and ooh! its tail was twirling round so fast.

"What's my name?" it said, as it gave her the skeins.

"Is that Solomon?" she said, pretending to be afraid.

"No! 't'ain't," it said, and it came further into the room.

"Well, is that Zebedee?" she said again.

"No! 't'ain't," said the impet. And then it laughed and twirled its tail until you could scarcely see it.

"Take time, woman," it said.

"Next guess, and you're mine."
And it stretched out its black hands
towards her.

Well, the girl backed away a step
or two. She looked at it, and then
she laughed and pointed a finger at
it and sang out:

"Nimmy nimmy not,
  Your name's Tom Tit Tot,"

Well, when the impet heard her,
it gave an awful shriek and away it
flew into the dark. She never saw it
again.